Vermillion Public Library

18 Church Street

Vermillion, SD 57069

(605) 677-7060

DEMCO

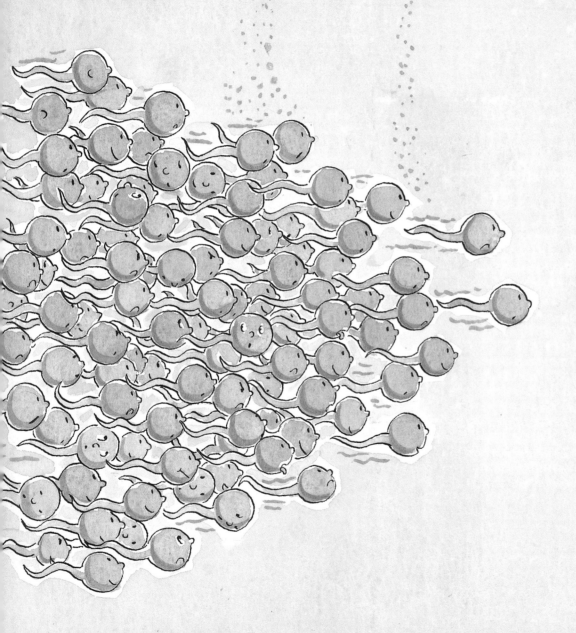

Where Willy Went...

Nicholas Allan

ALFRED A. KNOPF ❧ NEW YORK

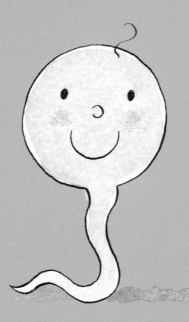

Willy was a little sperm.

He lived inside Mr. Browne . . .

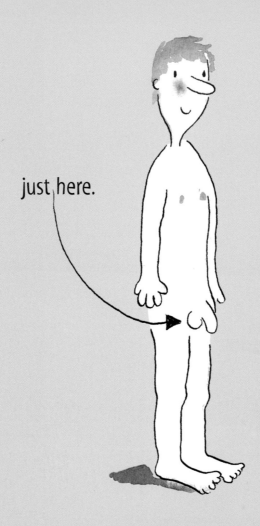

just here.

He lived with 300 million other sperm and they
all lived in Mr. Browne at the same address.

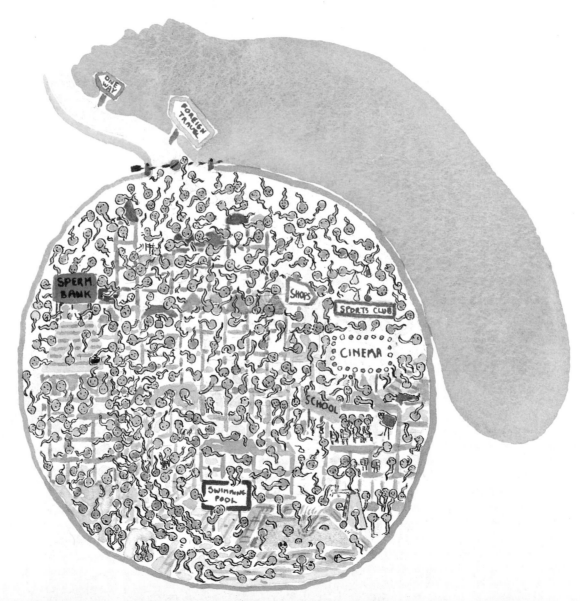

At school, Willy wasn't
very good at math.

But he was VERY good
at swimming.

So was Butch.

But there was only one prize—a beautiful egg.
The egg was inside Mrs. Browne ...

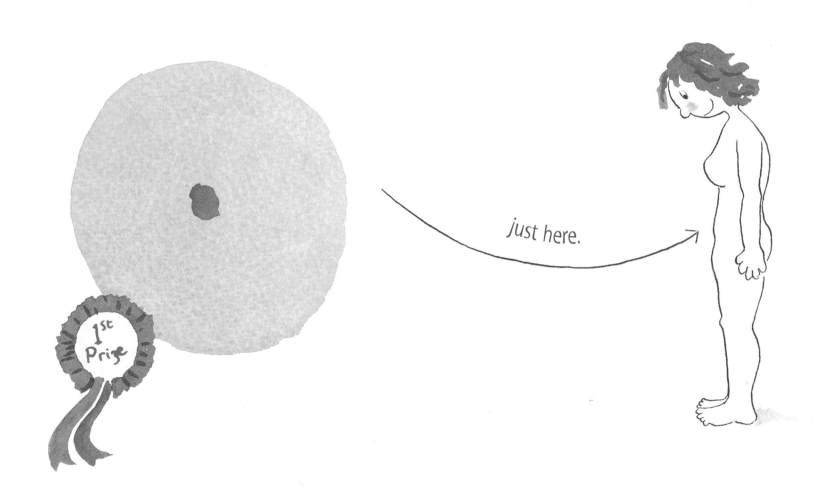

just here.

1st Prize

but so did all the other 300 million sperm . . .

and so did Butch.

Soon it would be time for the Great Swimming Race.

Willy practiced every day ...

LIFT

"If there are 300 million sperm in the race,
how many will you have to beat to win the egg?"
the teacher asked.

"Ten?" said Willy.
He wasn't very good at math, but he was VERY good at swimming.

At last the day of the Great Swimming Race arrived.
The teacher gave them all a pair of goggles.

And a number.

And two maps.

The first map showed
inside Mr. Browne.

The second map showed
inside Mrs. Browne.

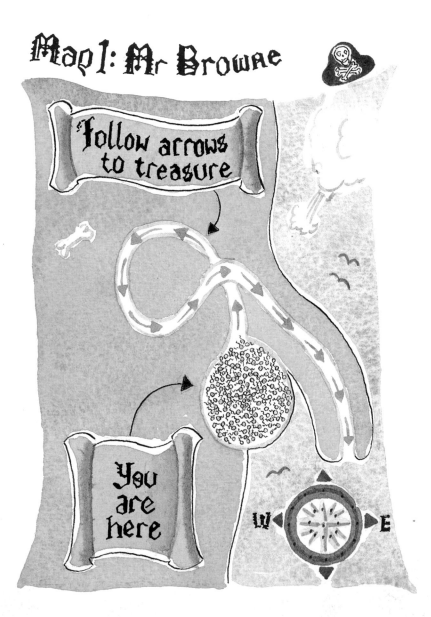

That very night Mr. and Mrs. Browne joined together.
The teacher cried, "Go!" and the Great Swimming Race began.

Willy swam and swam with all his strength. But so did Butch.

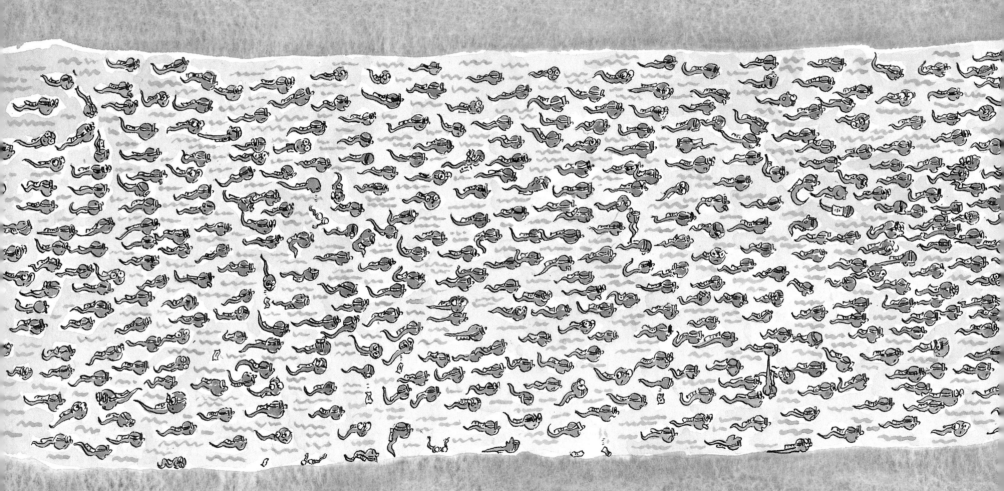

Butch was catching up. How much farther did Willy have to go?

Willy swam as if his life depended on it. Yet so did Butch.

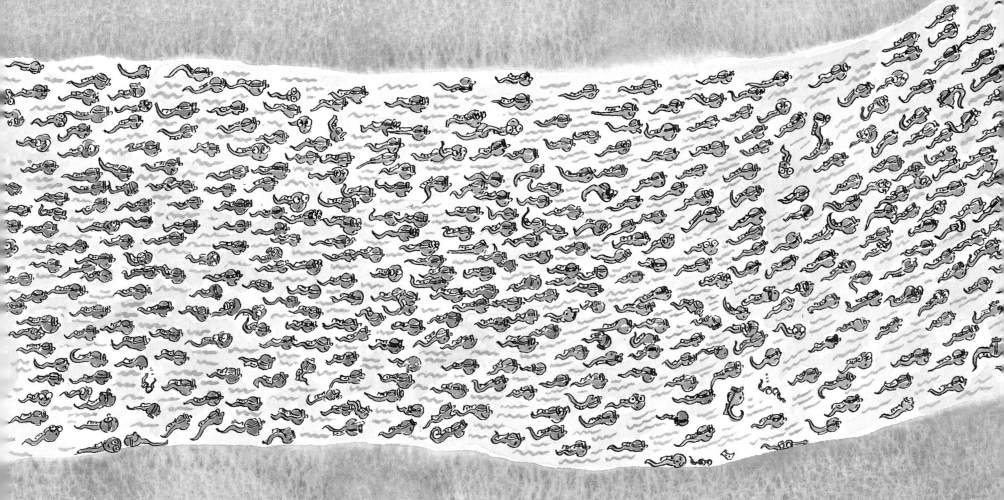

He didn't know. He wasn't very good at math...

... but he was the BEST at swimming! HURRAH!

FINISH

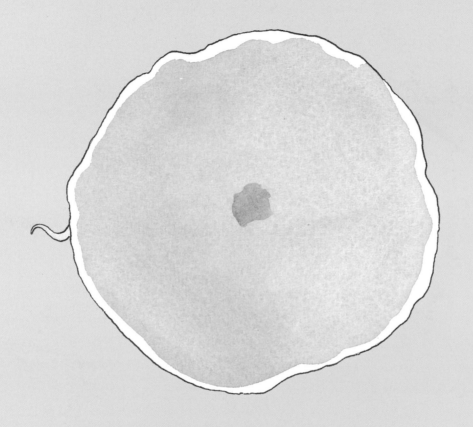

The egg was lovely and soft.
  Willy burrowed all the way in . . .

                              until he disappeared.

Then something
strange happened.

Something wonderful.

Something magical.

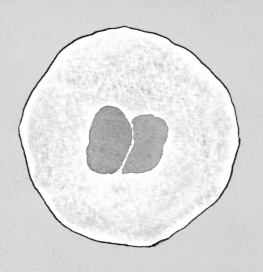

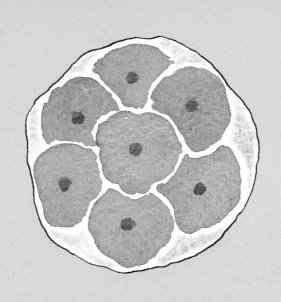

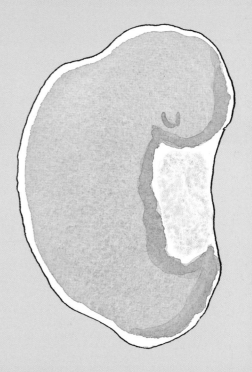

It grew and it grew until it grew bigger than the egg.

Something inside began to grow.

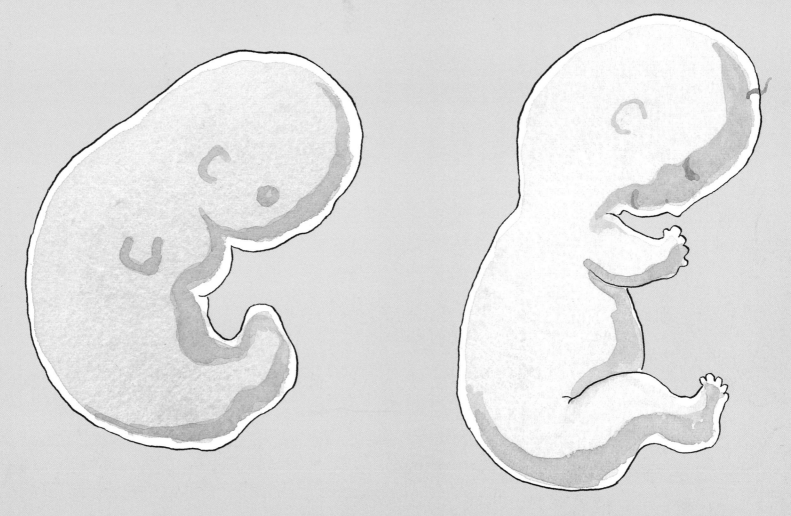

Then it grew some more until it grew bigger than Mrs. Browne's tummy.

So Mrs. Browne's tummy grew **bigger** instead.

It grew and it grew and it grew until . . .

the baby was born.

It was a little girl. They called her Edna.

Where had little Willy gone? Who knows?

But when Edna grew into a little girl and went to school . . .

she found she wasn't very good at math . . .

...but she was VERY good at swimming!

The End

To Rod Stewart

THIS IS A BORZOI BOOK PUBLISHED BY ALFRED A. KNOPF

Copyright © 2004 by Nicholas Allan

www.randomhouse.com/kids

Library of Congress Cataloging-in-Publication Data

Allan, Nicholas.

Where Willy went… / by Nicholas Allan.

p.   cm.

SUMMARY: A sperm named Willy, his main rival Butch, and millions of other sperm
take part in the Great Swimming Race to the body of Mrs. Browne.

ISBN 0-375-83030-8 (trade) — ISBN 0-375-93030-2 (lib. bdg.)

[1. Reproduction—Fiction.] I. Title.

PZ7.A412Wh 2004

[E]—dc22   2004040913

MANUFACTURED IN MALAYSIA

February 2005   First American Edition

10 9 8 7 6 5 4 3 2 1

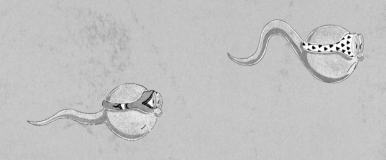